THE OLDEST WINGER IN TOWN

Old Buttspry Primary School

Name: Mabel Agnes Gladstone Muttley

Class: 5

Teacher: Mr Dibble

English	Written – Mabel would make better progress if she could be persuaded to use pen and paper instead of her slate. Spoken – Mabel is never at a loss for words. Unfortunately.
Maths	Mabel usually finishes the Numeracy Hour in ten minutes and spends the rest of the time polishing her abacus and tidying out her handbag.
History	Mabel has a vast knowledge of twentieth century history, but must get out of the habit of writing as if she was there at the time.
Drama	Mabel enjoys these sessions and makes imaginative use of her handbag.
Music	Since Mabel's first class singing lesson, when we all spent half an hour looking for a wounded cat, Mabel has been put in charge of the maracas.
Design Technology	All Mabel's work has been made with items she keeps in her handbag. Her scale model of Buckingham Palace made using hair curlers, corn plasters and an old corset has been much admired.
PE	Mabel is very sprightly and shows a lot of enthusiasm. However, she would do better if she put down her handbag.
General comments	Mabel has settled in quickly to Old Buttspry Primary and is a very popular member of the school. She obviously feels at home, as she wears her bedroom slippers in the classroom. Although Mabel shows a degree of independence well beyond her years, I am concerned about her need to cling to her handbag.
Head Teacher's comments	Well done, Mabel. Targets for next term – try not to take over Mr Dibble's history lessons. Remember that staff cannot be expected to come round at playtime with tea and biscuits. Try not to refer to members of staff as 'young so and so'.

Head of School .... Bleat. ....

Class Teacher .... Dibble ....

Days late   0

Days absent   0

THE OLDEST WINGER IN TOWN

BURCHETT & VOGLER

Illustrated by
Tim Archbold

BLOOMSBURY
CHILDREN'S
BOOKS

For Jackie Kirk and Georgia Thorp –
who could teach Councillor Scrimshanks
a thing or two about being a school governor

All rights reserved; no part of this publication may be
reproduced or transmitted by any means, electronic, mechanical,
photocopying or otherwise, without the prior permission
of the publisher

First published in Great Britain in 1999
Bloomsbury Publishing Plc, 38 Soho Square, London, W1V 5DF

Copyright © Text Janet Burchett and Sara Vogler 1999
Copyright © Illustrations Tim Archbold 1999

The moral right of the author has been asserted
A CIP catalogue record of this book is available from the
British Library

ISBN 0 7475 4265 1

Printed in England by Clays Ltd, St Ives plc

10 9 8 7 6 5 4 3 2 1

One

Class five were running round the Old Buttspry Primary School field. They were warming up for the highlight of the week – their football lesson.

The children jogged together in a cheerful clump. All except for Mabel Muttley. Mabel was lolloping along on her big flat feet, skinny legs sticking out of the bottom of her baggy white shorts, a string of beads round her neck and a huge handbag over her arm.

Her best friend, Jodie Bunn, sprinted up to her.

'Slow down, Mabel!' she panted. 'You're leaving us all behind!'

'Good footballers have to train hard,

dearie!' said Mabel, stopping to do some press-ups. 'And I'm definitely improving. I didn't lose any balls in the canal last week. If I carry on like this, Mr Dibble will have to put me in the school team next year.'

Jodie groaned at the thought. She was an ace striker and couldn't wait until she was in class six to be picked for the school side. Mabel, on the other hand, was totally useless at football. Unfortunately that didn't deter her.

'We never did this when I was a child,' she went on, as she sprang up and did some side lunges. 'Girls never played football then.'

'Shhh!' hissed Jodie, looking round in alarm. 'No one else must know you're a hundred and nine.'

'Hundred and ten in August,' Mabel reminded her proudly.

Nobody at Old Buttspry Primary School had any idea that Mabel was a century

older than the rest of class five. A hundred
years ago, Mabel had left Old Buttspry
Primary to work as a servant, but she'd
always promised herself that one day
she'd come back and finish her education.
And here she was. Her teacher, Mr Dibble,
and the head, Miss Bleat, had seen her
birth certificate and it seemed to be in
order, although Mabel did look rather
wrinkly for a nine-year-old. However,
when Mabel had shown the certificate to

them, her thumb had accidentally slipped over the year of her birth.

Mabel adjusted her glasses on her nose and trotted off again, handbag swinging. Jodie followed. They had just got to the far side of the field when Jodie suddenly saw the flash of metal studs. A leg with a football boot on the end stuck itself out from the bushes right in front of Mabel.

'Look out!' yelled Jodie.

Two

Without batting an eyelid, Mabel cleverly adjusted her stride and hurdled nimbly over the outstretched leg. There was a howl and it disappeared. Sidney Scrimshanks struggled out of the undergrowth, covered in nettle stings.

'You pushed me, Mabel Muttley!' he shouted after her. 'I'll get you for that!'

'Sorry, Sidney,' cackled Mabel over her shoulder. 'Must have caught you with me handbag.'

Sidney Scrimshanks, nastiest boy in class five and all-round bad egg, hated exercise – especially when others were having fun. He particularly loathed football. He usually wriggled out of it by pretending

he'd been struck by lightning, attacked by
a man-eating crocodile or got a dose of the
plague. If he ran out of excuses, he hid in a
bush.

Sidney's weaselly face turned purple
with fury. Mabel Muttley always got the
better of him. Why couldn't she have fallen
over his foot like most people and left him
alone in his bush?

He was just sneaking back amongst the leaves when Mabel marched over and took him by the hand.

'You can be me partner for shooting practice, Sidney,' she chortled.

'Not me,' growled Sidney. 'Go and pick on someone else.'

'Come on, boy!' said Mabel. 'Shake a leg, as Grandma Muttley said when she led the cancan on her eighty-first birthday.'

She delved in her handbag and pulled out a battered, old leather football.

The rest of the class sighed with relief. No one else wanted to be lumbered with spiteful Sidney.

Ten minutes later Sidney was lying exhausted on the field. It wasn't from saving Mabel's shots. Mabel had only scored once, and that was in someone else's goal. The rest of the time Sidney had

spent retrieving the heavy ball from under
the hedge, out of the ditch and between
the jaws of a passing Rottweiler.

Mr Dibble blew his whistle.

'Time for a game,' he called.

Sidney struggled to his feet and went to
sulk at the touchline. Jodie kicked off.

'Here I come,' cackled Mabel.

14

She zoomed down the pitch, baggy shirt flapping and handbag swinging as she zigzagged between the defenders. Soon it was just her and the goalie. The goalkeeper gave her a puzzled look.

'What are you doing, Mabel?' he said. 'The ball's up the other end.'

'So it is,' chortled Mabel. 'See you later.'

She scurried back up the pitch, arriving at the other goalmouth just as Jodie fired a scorcher of a shot. It was a certain goal.

'Well played, dearie!' called Mabel, waving her handbag in the air. The football hit the bag, knocked Mr Dibble on the head and bounced into the canal.

'Handball!' groaned Mr Dibble.

'Not exactly, sir,' said Mabel politely, helping him to his feet. 'I think you mean handbag-ball!'

'Cooee!' came a voice from the gate. It was Miss Bleat, the head teacher. She trotted across the field towards Mr Dibble. 'I have some exciting news for class five!'

Three

Class five gathered eagerly round the head teacher. Sidney sidled up, scowling.

'On Wednesday, the annual football match between Old Buttspry Primary and Wynalott Primary will take place,' announced Miss Bleat. 'Usually it is the school team from class six who plays this important fixture. But as you know, all the local year sixes are at Camp Collera and have been unexpectedly delayed. So perhaps you'd like to choose the team from class five, Mr Dibble?'

'Bless my bloomers!' exclaimed Mabel. 'That's us!'

'Indeed,' said Miss Bleat, beaming at her. 'I'm sorry it's such short notice, Mr Dibble, but I know you have some very promising young players.'

'I think she means me,' Mabel whispered to Jodie.

'Now let's see . . .' began Mr Dibble.

But Miss Bleat hadn't finished.

'Year after year,' she twittered on, 'we play football on this field, so kindly lent to us by Mrs Lavinia Lettuce. Year after year

we play an important match against
Wynalott Primary.' Her eyes narrowed and
she spoke through gritted teeth. 'And year
after year we lose!'

'We'll do our best . . .' said Mr Dibble.

'We'll do better than that!' squealed the
head. 'We'll thrash 'em!'

Class five's mouths dropped open.
They'd never seen their meek and mild

head teacher so excited. They'd never even heard her raise her voice before.

'Quite,' said Mr Dibble. 'If I might just . . .'

'They've beaten us for the last time!' bellowed Miss Bleat. 'We're going to win ten-nil. NO, TWENTY-NIL!'

'Thank you, Miss Bleat,' said Mr Dibble hurriedly. 'Shall I pick the team now?'

The head mopped her brow with a delicate lace hankie. 'Ah, yes . . . I do apologise. Don't know what came over me.'

The children clamoured round Mr Dibble. Mabel put her hand up.

'You'll be needing me, sir!' she called.

'Jodie will be captain,' said Mr Dibble,

ignoring her. 'And I'll have Bobby, Geoff, Roger . . .'

Mabel put both her hands up and jumped in the air. 'And me, sir!' she squeaked.

'Jackie, Rae, Georgina, and Gordon in goal,' continued Mr Dibble, trying not to look at Mabel.

Mabel stood on her handbag and wriggled desperately.

'I can play on the wing, sir!'

'Martin and Alan,' Mr Dibble went on regardless. 'And . . .'

'May I suggest Sidney,' twittered Miss Bleat. 'His father will expect him to be in the team,' she added in a whisper.

'I don't want to play!' whined Sidney.

'Don't be modest,' said Miss Bleat. 'Your father will be so proud. And what about this young girl?' she added, patting Mabel on the head. 'Such youthful enthusiasm should be rewarded.'

Mr Dibble's face fell. He looked at

Mabel, who beamed hopefully back up at him. 'I suppose she can be substitute,' he mumbled.

'Substitute!' exclaimed Mabel, shaking his hand vigorously. 'Thank you, sir! If only me mother could be there to see me.'

'Shame she can't,' said Jodie.

'It is, dearie,' agreed Mabel sadly. 'She always does kick-boxing on Wednesdays.'

'Listen, class five,' said Mr Dibble. 'We've only got two days to go, so the whole class will meet here again tomorrow lunchtime for a practice.'

Everyone began to chatter excitedly. Sidney glared round at the grinning faces.

'I don't want to be in the team!' he muttered. 'It's not fair. I'm going to tell my dad.'

Four

Next morning, a huge black chauffeur-driven car swept into the playground and pulled into the biggest parking space.

'I see Sidney's arrived,' said Jodie to Mabel as they walked through the school gates. 'Fancy being driven here when you only live fifty metres away!'

'That's the Scrimshankses for you,' replied Mabel. 'I remember when I was at this school with Sidney's great-great-grandfather. He used to get a servant to give him a piggyback here in the mornings.'

She pulled her sleeves up and began to scratch. 'Hang on a minute, Jodie,' she muttered. 'Me elbows are itching.'

Jodie stopped dead. She knew what that meant. Mabel's elbows always itched when there was trickery afoot.

'Sidney must be up to something,' said Jodie. 'Let's go and see.'

They sauntered up to the car and began a game of leapfrog round the next parking space. In the driver's seat they could see a huge chauffeur in a cap and dark glasses. Next to Sidney on the back seat sat a large man in a smart suit. It was Sidney's dad.

Cedric Scrimshanks, school governor and local councillor, considered himself to be the most important person at Old Buttspry Primary School – and so did everyone else. The cleaners even polished his shoes for him as he passed. He was forever interfering in school business, although since Mabel had arrived, things didn't always turn out as he intended.

Through the open car window, Mabel and Jodie could hear Sidney whining.

'Everyone's going on about this football match, Dad,' he whinged, 'and I'm in the team.'

'Well done, Sidney,' came Councillor Scrimshanks's heavy voice. 'But if my boy's in the team he should be captain. I'll speak to Mr Dibble.'

'I don't want to be in the team at all, Dad!' screeched Sidney. 'I hate football and I've got to do loads of practice on that horrible field and every time I hide in the bushes that stupid Mabel Muttley finds me and it's not fair!'

'If my boy doesn't want to play football,' said Councillor Scrimshanks, 'he doesn't have to play football. I'll tell Miss Bleat.'

'But Dad!' wailed Sidney. 'You know I hate it when everyone else is having a good time and I'm left out. I wish someone would dig up that field – then there won't be any more football ever!'

'If my boy doesn't want any more football, there won't be any more football.

You've given me an idea, Sidney. Something that'll help you and my business at the same time. Close the windows, Fat Frank. I don't want anyone else to hear this.'

Mr Scrimshanks's driver pushed a button and the tinted windows of the limousine slid smoothly up. Mabel and Jodie leapfrogged off round the corner towards their classroom.

'Old Scrimshanks is going to spoil our fun as usual,' said Jodie. 'I was so looking forward to being captain of the football team.'

'And so you shall be!' declared Mabel, with a determined shake of her handbag. 'And I'll be substitute – or my name's not Mabel Agnes Gladstone Muttley.'

Five

At lunchtime, class five were on the field helping the team to practise for the match tomorrow.

Jodie's heart wasn't in it. She knew that Councillor Scrimshanks was hatching

some awful plan. Mabel was her usual merry self.

'On me head, Roger . . . Look out, Sidney! . . . Ooops! . . . Won't be a minute, Jodie. Just got to get the ball out of that tree . . . Try and save this one, Gordon . . . Oh I am sorry, Mr Dibble sir. I was aiming for the goal.'

Miss Bleat was on the touchline. Suddenly the ball shot off the pitch, narrowly missing her head. Mabel came scampering after it.

'I'm on form today, Miss Bleat!' she called as she dived into a hedge to retrieve the ball. She was rummaging about in the undergrowth when she heard heavy footsteps and a familiar voice.

'Ah, Miss Bleat.' It was Sidney's dad. 'I've been looking for you all morning.'

'You've come at the right moment, Councillor Scrimshanks,' twittered the head teacher. 'The football team is practising for the Big Match tomorrow.'

'That's why I'm here,' said Councillor Scrimshanks solemnly. 'I am the bearer of bad news. Mrs Lettuce is selling the school field today. We won't be able to use it any more.'

'That's terrible!' squealed Miss Bleat. 'If we lose the field the match cannot take place. I must go and see Lavinia Lettuce at once.'

'Don't worry, Miss Bleat,' said Sidney's dad soothingly. 'As school governor, it's *my* place to talk to her. I'll soon sort out the

fate of the field – and just to be sure, I'll
have it put in writing.'

'Thank you, Councillor Scrimshanks,'
panted Miss Bleat, fanning herself with a
shin pad. 'What would we do without
you?'

Mabel scrambled out of the hedge
backwards, clutching the football. She
marched up to Councillor Scrimshanks
and shook him vigorously by the hand.

'Nice to see you supporting the school team, sir,' she cackled, depositing bits of hedge all over him.

Sidney's dad backed away as if she was a highly poisonous tarantula. He brushed the leaves off his suit.

'Dad!' yelled Sidney, running over. 'Can I stop playing now, Dad?'

Councillor Scrimshanks gave a nervous laugh. 'Course not, son. Carry on with the game.'

'But Dad,' wailed Sidney, 'you said there wouldn't be any more football after Mrs Lettuce sells the field . . .'

'No, Sidney,' spluttered his father, going pink. 'I said there wouldn't be any more football *if* she sells the field.' He shoved Sidney quickly back on to the pitch and turned to the head. 'I've got an important meeting now. I'll see Mrs Lettuce straight after school.'

He lumbered off towards the gate. Mabel scratched her elbows.

'There's more to this than meets the eye,'
she muttered to herself, 'as Grandma
Muttley said when she spotted the tip of a
tiger's tail in the jungle. I think me and
Jodie had better get to Mrs Lettuce first.'

Six

Mabel and Jodie skidded to a halt at the gate of Mrs Lettuce's rambling old farmhouse. As soon as the bell had gone for the end of school, they'd run all the way.

'Old Scrimshanks has beaten us to it,' gasped Jodie, pointing down the drive.

Councillor Scrimshanks's black limousine was parked in front of the house, with Fat Frank asleep in the driver's seat.

'Only one thing to do, dearie!' said Mabel firmly. 'We're going in.'

They tiptoed past the snoring driver and went up to the door. Mabel grasped the brass door knocker and gave it a hefty rap.

The door swung open and a tall, jolly woman stood in front of them. Mabel stepped forwards and shook her hand.

'You must be Mrs Lettuce,' she said politely. 'I'm Mabel and this is Jodie. We've come from Old Buttspry Primary School . . .'

'Come in, children,' beamed Lavinia Lettuce. 'The more the merrier. I expect you've come about the football. Your school governor's already here. He's been telling me all about it.'

She led the way down a long hall and into a lounge. Councillor Scrimshanks was sitting in the biggest armchair, clutching a tea plate and a piece of paper. Sidney was in the corner, squatting at the feet of a fearsome suit of armour and stuffing his face with macaroons.

'Good afternoon, Councillor Scrimshanks,' said Mabel cheerfully.

Sidney's dad choked on his rock cake.

Mrs Lettuce turned to Mabel and Jodie.

'You youngsters at Old Buttspry don't know how lucky you are having Councillor Scrimshanks around.'

'Oh yes we do!' piped up Mabel.

'In fact,' Mrs Lettuce went on, 'he's so keen to help the school that he wants to make sure you can always use my field for your football. He suggests I put my promise in writing. Isn't that jolly! Now where's the paper for me to sign? Pass the cakes round, girls.'

Councillor Scrimshanks laid the paper ceremoniously on the table and placed his best gold pen beside it. The top of the paper was folded over.

'We've got it wrong, Mabel,' whispered Jodie as she caught sight of the words on the document. 'It looks as if the field's safe. We'd better go.'

But Mabel was too busy scratching her elbows. Then she put down her handbag and picked up the plate of scones. As she

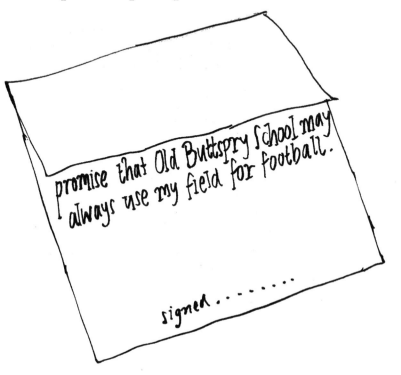

promise that Old Buttspry School may always use my field for football.

signed . . . .

held it out to Councillor Scrimshanks she appeared to stumble. The jam-covered scones flew through the air and landed on his suit where they slowly slithered down into his lap.

'Silly me!' cackled Mabel, offering him a hankie. 'Must have tripped over me own handbag!'

Sidney's dad leapt to his feet and began to scrub frantically at his jacket. 'Give us a hand, son!' he ordered.

'But I don't like jam, Dad!' whined Sidney, not budging.

Mabel looked round. Lavinia Lettuce was sponging butter smears off Councillor Scrimshanks's jacket and Sidney was busy testing the points of a mace that hung on the armour. She quickly unfolded the piece of paper that lay on the table.

Jodie gasped as they read the whole document.

Seven

Mabel quickly folded the paper up again,
just as Lavinia Lettuce put down her
sponge and picked up Councillor
Scrimshanks's gold pen.

I, Mrs Lavinia Lettuce, hereby sell my
field to C. S. Properties for houses
to be built there, and so take back my
promise that Old Buttspry School may
always use my field for football.

signed . . . .

'I'll sign this for you,' she said. 'Then you can be off to the dry-cleaners.'

Jodie looked desperately at Mabel. If Mrs Lettuce signed the paper, the field would be lost and there would be no more football at Old Buttspry School. But Mabel was marching towards the door, her handbag firmly over her arm.

'Thank you for the scones, Mrs Lettuce,' she said. 'Now we know the field's in safe hands, we can go.'

'But Mabel . . .' began Jodie.

'That's right, girls,' said Councillor Scrimshanks eagerly. 'On your way.'

As Mabel passed Sidney he reached out to poke her with the mace. The suit of armour rocked on its stand and crashed down, covering Sidney in pieces of metal.

'Mind Sir Cuthbert!' gasped Mrs Lettuce, dropping the gold pen on the floor and rushing over.

'Oops!' cackled Mabel, hopping nimbly behind the table. 'Must have caught him

with me handbag.' She picked up the
pen.

'Dad!' yelled Sidney, from under the pile.
'Get me out!'

'Don't be impatient, son,' said Councillor
Scrimshanks. 'Got important things to do
first.' He lumbered over to the table and
placed a heavy hand over the folded
paper.

signed..........

'I'll keep it still for you, Mrs Lettuce, if you'd care to sign now.'

'Here's the pen,' said Mabel, holding it out.

'But we mustn't let her sign it,' whispered Jodie frantically.

'Nonsense, dearie,' Mabel said loudly. 'Councillor Scrimshanks is right. We must have it all in writing.'

Lavinia Lettuce took the pen and signed the document with a flourish.

Eight

It was Wednesday. The big match was due to start in five minutes and the whole school had come to watch. The Wynalott Primary players were in a huddle on the

far side of the field. Mabel and Jodie were warming up with their team.

'I've chopped the oranges for half-time,' Mabel told Jodie as she jogged on the spot, handbag over her arm. 'I've polished all the boots and I'm ready to cheer. Can't wait for kick-off.'

'I keep telling you, Mabel,' sighed Jodie. 'There's not going to be a kick-off. Councillor Scrimshanks will be here any minute to tell us the field's been sold.'

'Could be,' said Mabel with a cheerful grin. 'Wait and see, dearie.'

Mr Dibble called the children over.

'Miss Bleat would like to say a few words,' he announced. He helped the excited head teacher on to a wobbly chair and handed her a loud hailer. Everyone gathered round – except for Sidney, who skulked at the back, checking his watch anxiously.

'Attention, everyone . . .' began Miss Bleat through the loud hailer.

At that moment, Councillor Scrimshanks
burst through the gate and swaggered
over. Fat Frank followed, carrying a leather
briefcase.

'Told you so,' Jodie muttered to Mabel.

'Prepare yourself for a shock, Miss Bleat,'
said Councillor Scrimshanks solemnly.
'The football match cannot take place!'

The team gasped in horror and Miss Bleat tottered dangerously on her chair.

'I am sorry to tell you that Mrs Lettuce has sold the field,' he continued. 'I have a copy of the contract here.' He clicked his fingers and Fat Frank opened the briefcase. Councillor Scrimshanks pulled out a piece of paper and thrust it under the head's nose. 'The field is now owned by C. S. properties – whatever that is.'

'You know what that is, Dad!' piped up Sidney, pushing forwards. 'It stands for Cedric Scrim . . .'

'Shut up, Sidney!' hissed his dad. 'We must all leave the field immediately, Miss Bleat. The bulldozers are on their way. There will be no more football at Old Buttspry Primary School.'

Nine

'No more football!' exclaimed Mr Dibble.

There were gasps of disbelief from the crowd.

'I can't tell you how sorry I am,' said Councillor Scrimshanks, 'and Sidney's beside himself with grief. Aren't you, Sidney?'

'Yes, Dad!' smirked Sidney, with a huge grin on his face.

Miss Bleat stood on her chair, rigid with shock, the paper in her hand.

'Do look at it, Miss Bleat!' piped up Mabel. 'You should always check the small print.'

With a glum expression, the head began to read.

47

'Wait a minute!' she squealed suddenly. 'There may be hope yet!' She flapped the document in excitement.

'I don't think so,' said Councillor Scrimshanks. 'I wrote the contract . . . er . . . I mean, I *read* the contract most carefully.'

'But listen to this!' squeaked the head.

I, Mrs Lavinia Lettuce hereby sell my field to C.S. Properties for houses to be built there, and so take back my promise that Old Buttspry School may always use my field for football. However if they win their match on Wednesday, I will never sell the field to anyone and Old Buttspry school can play there forever.

signed. Lavinia Lettuce

'Let me see that!' snarled Councillor Scrimshanks, snatching the document and nearly pulling the head teacher off her chair. As he read it, his face turned purple and he glared at Mabel and Jodie.

Mabel grinned at him. 'Isn't that good news, sir!'

Jodie looked at her wrinkly friend.

'You're amazing, Mabel,' she whispered. 'It was you who put those extra words in. How did you do it without anyone seeing?'

'Easy as winking, dearie!' Mabel whispered back. 'I slipped them in when Sir Cuthbert fell on Sidney.'

Sidney pulled at his father's sleeve.

'I don't want to play football, Dad!' he wailed. 'You said I wouldn't have to.'

'Listen, son,' said Councillor Scrimshanks. He whispered something into his ear. Sidney's eyes lit up.

'I won't let you down, Dad,' he

sniggered, rubbing his hands with evil glee
as he ran on to the pitch.

Jodie watched him suspiciously. She'd
never seen Sidney eager to play football
before.

The head teacher was hopping up and
down on her chair.

'We're in with a chance!' she squeaked.
'We've got a solid defence, a strong

midfield and fast strikers. We can save the field!'

'Calm yourself, Miss Bleat,' said Councillor Scrimshanks firmly. 'Old Buttspry have never beaten Wynalott Primary before.'

Mabel rummaged in her handbag and pulled out an old football rattle. She winked at Councillor Scrimshanks.

'There's a first time for everything, sir, as Grandma Muttley said when she went hang-gliding over the Grand Canyon at ninety-eight.' She waved the rattle round her head with a deafening clatter. 'Come on, Old Buttspry!'

The whistle blew and Old Buttspry kicked off. The crowd roared. They knew that this was the most important match the school had ever played.

Mabel hopped about on the touchline, waving her rattle and her handbag. Miss Bleat bit her nails and feebly flapped a school scarf. Fat Frank fetched Councillor Scrimshanks an armchair from the staffroom and settled down for a snooze on the grass.

To Councillor Scrimshanks's dismay, Old Buttspry got off to a good start. As soon as Jodie gained possession of the ball, she did a brilliant run, dodging defenders as she went. Before Wynalott could do anything about it she'd reached their penalty area.

She was about to shoot when Sidney suddenly appeared beside her.

'My ball!' he shouted, sticking his foot out.

Jodie crashed to the ground and the Wynalott goalie gathered up the ball.

'Silly me!' sniggered Sidney.

'Take him off!' shrieked Mabel from the touchline. 'I'll play instead.'

'Not Sidney's fault!' called Councillor Scrimshanks. 'The girl should look where she's going.'

Jodie dragged herself to her feet. So that's what Sidney was up to. He was out to make sure Old Buttspry lost the match – and the field.

Ten

At half-time, Old Buttspry were one nil down.

The team were flopped on the grass – all except Sidney, who was perched on the side of his father's armchair enjoying

diversionary tactics

a bottle of cola and an iced bun.

'How am I doing, Dad?' he whispered.

'Brilliant, son!' said his father in a loud voice. 'Nice diversionary tactics, good tackles and clever footwork.' He lowered his voice. 'Keep it up and the field will be ours!'

Mabel scurried around, handing out pieces of orange. Then she delved in her handbag and produced a huge tube of ointment.

'How's your leg, Jodie? Want some

Good tackles   Clever footwork

Dr Edison's Embrocation rubbed in? It always came in handy at the Olympic games,' she whispered.

'Keep your peckers up!' she cackled to the team as she rubbed the foul-smelling cream into Jodie's knee. 'We just need a couple of goals and the field will be ours. Anyone want a rest? I'm keen for a game.'

She started warming up.

'No thanks, Mabel,' sighed Jodie. 'It's

bad enough having Sidney on the pitch without you as well.'

'Wash your mouth out, girl!' exclaimed Mabel. 'I'm an asset to Old Buttspry.'

Jodie and her team dragged themselves back on to the pitch for the second half. They needed two goals to win the match and there seemed to be no hope of getting them. And then, just when it looked as if things couldn't get any worse, Martin's ankle got in the way of Sidney's boot and Martin limped off injured.

'My big moment!' cackled Mabel as she tore off her cardigan and adjusted her shin pads.

She scampered on to the pitch, handbag over her arm, and beads rattling. The team looked horrified and Jodie groaned.

'I'll play on the wing, sir!' called Mabel.

Mr Dibble put his head in his hands.

Mabel popped up everywhere on the field. Wynalott Primary were gobsmacked. The sight of the small, skinny figure

scuttling amongst them with her handbag
put them right off their game.

Suddenly Jodie found herself unmarked
and with the ball at her feet. She dodged
skilfully round the dazed defenders and
made for goal. The supporters cheered.
This could be the equaliser! Then Jodie
saw Sidney. He was making a beeline for
her and he had a nasty look on his face. As
he came alongside, he reached out a
sneaky hand to grab her shirt. Jodie's heart
sank.

And then suddenly he was gone. Jodie
took her chance. She charged into the
penalty area and blasted the ball at the
goal. It sailed over the goalie's head and
into the back of the net. One-all! The crowd
went wild. Old Buttspry were in with a
chance!

As Jodie jogged back for Wynalott's kick-
off she passed Sidney. He was running
furiously on the spot with Mabel behind
him.

'Bless my bloomers, Sidney,' cackled
Mabel, winking at Jodie. 'Your shorts seem
to be caught on the clasp of me handbag.
Soon have you free . . . Whoops! Looks like
I've snapped your elastic!'

Sidney made a desperate grab for his
shorts.

'Come on, Old Buttspry!' called Miss
Bleat from her chair. 'There's only five

minutes to the final whistle and we need another goal. THE FUTURE OF FOOTBALL DEPENDS ON IT!'

Now at last the team felt they could win. But the seconds were ticking away. Councillor Scrimshanks leant back in his chair with a smug smile on his face. A draw would not be enough to save the field. He clicked his fingers and Fat Frank woke up and handed him a mobile phone.

'Scrimshanks here,' he said in a low voice. 'Send them in now.'

There was a loud rumbling and four bulldozers, with C. S. Properties on the side, drove up to the field. All the players on the pitch stopped and stared. Miss Bleat picked up her loud hailer.

'KEEP PLAYING!' she screamed. 'THERE'S STILL ONE MINUTE AND FIFTY-FIVE SECONDS TO GO!'

Old Buttspry sprang into action. Jodie won the ball and thumped it desperately up the pitch. It landed bang in the middle of the Wynalott penalty area. There were only two players near it: the Wynalott goalie and Mabel Muttley. Sidney made to run towards Mabel. He was going to get the ball off her – and have some fun into the bargain. Unfortunately he forgot to hold on to his shorts. They dropped round his feet and he fell flat on his face.

Mabel pounced on the ball and swung her leg enthusiastically towards the goal. The ball flew high in the air. The referee checked his watch and put the whistle in his mouth.

Eleven

A groan of dismay went round the Old Buttspry supporters as the ball flew backwards over Mabel's head.

But to everyone's astonishment, Mabel bent her leg nimbly behind her, caught the ball on her heel, flicked it forwards and on to her knee. Then she tapped it up on to her shoulder, nudged it into the air and headed it at the goal. The Wynalott goalie just stood there open mouthed as the ball sailed into the back of the net.

The referee blew his whistle. The supporters raced on to the pitch, waving their scarves and yelling with delight. Old Buttspry School had won the football match!

'The field is saved!' shrieked Miss Bleat as she fell off her chair in excitement.

Jodie rushed up to Mabel and gave her a hug.

'That was amazing ball skill!' she gasped. 'How did you do it?'

'Simple, dearie,' cackled Mabel. 'I suddenly remembered me Muttley Apple Catching Manoeuvre. It always came in useful when I went fruit picking.'

Councillor Scrimshanks was standing on the touchline looking sick.

'Send the bulldozers away, Fat Frank,' he muttered. He pulled out the letter that Lavinia Lettuce had signed and went to tear it up. All at once it was snatched from his hands.

'I think Miss Bleat should have that, sir,' chortled Mabel, waving it at him from high up on the shoulders of her team-mates.

Sidney staggered to his feet, clutching his shorts.

'Dad!' he squealed. 'It's not fair, Dad! My shorts are busted and we've still got the field and I've got to play football for ever and . . .' He was trampled by the victory marchers carrying Mabel and her handbag round the pitch.

'One thing's for certain, Jodie,' cackled Mabel as the supporters gathered round, yelling her name. 'The school team can't do without me next year.'